This Book Has Ghosts in It

Dawn Vogel

ISBN-13: 978-1-948280-49-5

CONTENTS

CONTENT NOTES

Most pieces in this collection touch on death and/or murder in some way (without graphic details). Some other potential content notes are below.

"Homecoming" includes cult-like behavior.

"Progress" references suicide.

"Hollow" involves mental instability and a perceived endangered child.

"Queen of the Roller Disco" involves accidental death and injury from normal activities.

"Glaistig" involves murder by a romantic partner.

"The House" involves separation of a person and her pet.

"Things Cats Put in Their Mouths" involves pets in potential danger.

"Glitch Fog" involves zombies.

HOMECOMING

Carolyn hadn't been back to Whitepine Harbor in ten years, and everything seemed different from her memories. It went beyond shops changing names or exterior paint colors, or the models of cars parked in driveways. It was like her brain had reconfigured the town with equal parts nostalgia and decrepitude. The beach, at least, looked nicer than she remembered.

The house she had rented for the long weekend, however, was far more run down than it had appeared on the vacation rental site.

"Carolyn? Carolyn Wilder?" A woman, maybe in her early forties, a decade and change older than Carolyn, ran across the next-door backyard waving.

"That's me." Carolyn racked her brain for the woman's name, but nothing came to her. Whitepine Harbor was small enough that she'd known everyone when she lived there, but this woman was a blank.

"Hi, sorry, I'm Bonnie Harkins. Mrs. Dawson asked me to catch you when you got here. She, uh ... well, I guess you haven't heard about Anthony passing away."

"Mr. Dawson? I thought he—"

"No, no, Anthony Junior."

Carolyn blinked. "You mean Tony."

Bonnie nodded. "May he rest in peace."

"Wow. Uh, I used to babysit him." Carolyn glanced at the rental house. "Oh, gosh, should I find a different place?"

"No, no," Bonnie said, handing Carolyn a single key on a coiled plastic circle keyring she pulled from her wrist. "Mrs. Dawson wants you to stay here still. She was just sorry she couldn't make it over to see you herself."

"I should send her my condolences," Carolyn said. "Do you know what happened?"

"Drowning."

The single word struck Carolyn, knocking the breath out of her lungs and leaving her unable to speak. Tony had been a good swimmer—most people in Whitepine Harbor learned to swim when they were young. The town didn't have a pool, but with the northern Pacific Ocean right there at their doorstep, not knowing how to swim was a liability. Even after years away, she still swam when she had the chance, though in indoor pools these days.

"So, Mrs. Dawson said you're a digital nomad?" Bonnie asked. "What's that mean, exactly?"

"Oh, just that I work wherever I go," Carolyn replied, shrugging. "It's ... I guess it's a lot more common in bigger cities. But I work in data analysis, and you can do that from anywhere with an internet connection."

"That sounds glamorous! The Wi-Fi here should work, but there's a coffee shop a couple of blocks away, too."

"Coffee shop? That's new."

"Yeah, it opened a few years back, I guess. I'm not from around here. My husband's family is."

"Harkins, you said? I remember Mr. Harkins, the biology teacher."

"That's right. I married Jimmy, his youngest son."

Carolyn nodded. "Oh, yeah, I think I remember him too. He moved away for a while?"

"Yep, Northern California. Met me, we had a couple kids. Moved back after his mom passed."

"Oh, I'm sorry to hear it."

Bonnie nodded. "Thanks. Anyway, let me show you around the house, okay?"

Carolyn glanced at the house. "There's not much to see, is there?"

"Well, you know Mrs. Dawson, she just wants to make sure you feel at home. After all, it's your big homecoming, right?"

"Ten-year reunion, but yeah, I guess it's homecoming too." Carolyn opened the back door into the rental and stepped inside.

The kitchen was tiny, with a table for two, and its vinyl flooring stopped abruptly at the brown shag carpet of the living room. The layout was exactly like her parents' house had been—the two bedrooms would be on the front of the house, facing the ocean, with the front door between them and the bathroom tucked at the end of the hall nearest the kitchen.

But Bonnie insisted on showing Carolyn around, and she followed along, nodding as she went. The house was plenty big enough for just her—she wouldn't even need the second bedroom. They wound back around to the living room in no time.

Carolyn paused as her gaze caught on something propped against a lamp on an end table. It looked like a bone white replica of a distorted human face. She recoiled. "What's that?"

"Oh, that's a driftwood mask," Bonnie said. "Well, they weren't designed to be masks. One of the old lumber mills had a chute that carried their waste wood out to the ocean. It's all been tumbling around out there for decades, but in the past couple of years, they've been washing up on the beach now and then. It's white pine, you know, like the town name, and I guess the holes in them are where the knots used to be."

"Wow. Kinda creepy."

"I think they're kinda cute. They've all got different expressions, just like people."

"If you say so," Carolyn said. "Um, anyway, thanks for the tour and the tip on the coffee shop. But—" She pointed back toward the hallway. "I've been on the road for hours. Nature beckons."

"Oh, sorry, don't let me keep you! I'll get out of your hair, but if you need anything, I'm just two houses down, four-oh-eight. I'd sooner you come pester me than Mrs. Dawson, okay?"

"Thank you," Carolyn said.

As Bonnie headed out, Carolyn looked at the mask again. But she hadn't been making an excuse to get Bonnie to leave. She headed for the bathroom without giving the mask another thought.

~

Carolyn was glad she'd brought a few groceries with her from her last short-term rental in Seattle. The Whitepine Harbor grocery store was as dismal as she remembered it. This time of year, there was some fresh produce, so long as you didn't mind apples, gourds, or greens of dubious quality. And there was always fish and shellfish, locally caught. She'd never learned to cook fish, definitely not the sort you needed to skin and debone yourself. She'd settled on a bit of deli meat and cheese to round out a charcuterie board pieced together from what she'd brought with her and a bottle of wine she'd picked up at a roadside tasting room on the way out.

Now, sitting on the front porch where she'd watched the sun set as she ate, she shivered as the brine-scented breeze wafted across her. Wisps of fog came with it, shrouding the beach in pale grays under the amber glow of the streetlights. Autumn in Washington was rarely beach season, and today was no exception. She drained her wine glass and collected the dishes she'd brought out to the porch.

Back in the house, the chill breeze still followed her, and she made her way from room to room, closing windows as she went. Mrs. Dawson—or maybe Bonnie—had opened everything up to air the place out, but it seemed plenty aired out to Carolyn.

She didn't bother to turn the light on in the spare bedroom as she went to close the window there. Looking out the window and across the street, motion caught her gaze.

Darker shapes moved amongst the fog, roughly human sized. Probably teenagers out drinking, she thought with a grin. She'd been one of those teenagers, once upon a time. And as long as they weren't loud about it, she couldn't begrudge them the one activity Whitepine Harbor provided after dark.

But she was an adult now, not needing to sneak out to drink. She poured herself another glass of wine to enjoy within the warmth of the house.

~

The sign at the coffee shop read "Harbor Fog," with an artistic swirl of steam from a cup of coffee wreathing the words. Carolyn thought she recognized the style, but it wasn't until she went inside and saw her high school best friend, Elodie, working the cash register, that she was certain.

"El! Oh my gosh! Hi!"

"Carolyn?" Elodie arched one slender dark eyebrow. "What are you ... you came back for homecoming?"

"And the reunion," Carolyn said, eyeing Elodie's appearance. Her hair had always been dark, but the black lipstick and heavy eyeliner was new, as was the solid black outfit. "Um, are you in mourning?"

Elodie glanced down. "No. Black hides the coffee stains."

"Oh, right. Barista." Carolyn bit her lip as she looked up at the menu. "What's good?"

"How much caffeine do you want?"

"Some?" Carolyn yawned. "Okay, a lot."

"Our signature drink is a flat white espresso, topped with whipped cream, sea salt, and cinnamon. It's the Harbor Fog, same as the shop."

"Sounds perfect." Carolyn looked around, surprised there weren't more patrons in the coffee shop. But at least it meant she could catch up with Elodie. "So how'd you end up here?"

"My other options were grocery store checker, gas station attendant, or waitress," Elodie muttered as she began making the drink. "Not a lot going on here in Whitepine Harbor."

"I'm surprised you didn't move away, I guess."

"Moving away requires money, Care. My family's not loaded."

Carolyn blushed. Her mom had passed away from aggressive breast cancer the autumn after Carolyn and Elodie had graduated from high school. Her life insurance policy had paid out well enough for Carolyn and her dad to move away, long before the town's economy bottomed out. "Sorry, I didn't—"

"It's fine, whatever. Someday I'll get out of here. Anyway, we can't all be hashtag digital nomad."

"What?"

"Your Instagram. Most used hashtag." Elodie grabbed the whipped cream, just a can from the grocery store rather than a fancy dispenser, and went to work on Carolyn's drink.

When the pressurized air stopped, Carolyn grinned. "I didn't know you followed me on Insta! What's your username?"

"I don't have one." Elodie finished the drink with a shake from each of two cannisters, the first dappling the whipped cream with rust-colored specks and the second with white flakes of salt. "Your posts are public."

"Right." Carolyn nodded as she accepted the drink. "Do you want to catch up later?"

Elodie shifted her focus to something behind the counter, not making eye contact with Carolyn. "I'll have to check my schedule."

"Well, if not tonight, then maybe tomorrow at the Seaside? Or Friday at the reunion?"

"Maybe, yeah." The bell on the coffee shop door jangled, and Elodie's gaze fixed on the people coming in. "Business."

"Right." Carolyn took her drink to a small table and snapped a photo of it before putting the lid on her paper cup. Before she sat, she noticed her phone was getting no bars of signal, and there were no available wireless networks. Glancing up at Elodie, she noticed the sign on the Wi-Fi router reading "Out of service." With a sigh, Carolyn grabbed a cardboard sleeve for her cup and slipped past the group of customers perusing the coffee shop menu.

~

After a long day of analyzing data, Carolyn unwound watching humorous videos on her laptop, since the house TV only got a couple of staticky channels. A rental house this close to the beach was meant for people who wanted to enjoy the outdoors, not sit inside all day and night.

A strange thwapping made her pause the video she was watching, trying to determine if it was background noise in the video or something else. The sound continued, so she set her laptop aside and walked around inside the house, trying to find the source.

It was loudest in the bedroom she was staying in, selected for its proximity to the bathroom—no sense in stumbling down the whole hall for a morning shower—but it didn't seem to be anything within the room itself. She peered out the window toward the beach, foggy yet again, with fingers of mist and darkness interweaving.

But there were voices, too, warped and distorted. Carolyn headed out onto the porch, then onto the sidewalk lining the narrow street between the houses and the beach.

"Hello?" she called out.

Multiple voices jumbled together, harsh whispers and panicked yelps, until a single figure emerged from the fog. "Carolyn Wilder?"

Carolyn peered at the familiar face until it clicked. "Scott George?" He still looked like he had at graduation, all sandy blonde hair framing his sun-kissed skin. He looked like a California surfer, though she knew his tan was just his natural coloration and his musculature was from football.

"Yeah!" Scott said, his face beaming as he jogged to the middle of the street. "Welcome back! Just couldn't stay away, am I right?"

"Thanks. Just here for the reunion, you know."

"Right, yep." He glanced behind him. "We're just getting ready for the big game!"

"Oh, right, the homecoming game." Carolyn frowned. "On the beach?"

"Hazing the freshies," Scott replied. "It's tradition, the night before. So, how have you been?"

"Fine, thanks," she said. "I don't mean to be a stick in the mud, but how late does this hazing thing go?"

"Oh, I dunno, a few hours. But we didn't realize anyone was staying in the rental. We'll move it farther out. It's cool."

"Great, thanks. Uh, I guess I'll see you at the reunion?"

"I'll be at the Seaside tomorrow, after the game," Scott said. "Buy you a drink?"

Carolyn nodded. "Yeah, sure. See you then." She headed back into the house, pausing to watch Scott and the other guys he was hanging out with retreat farther into the mist.

Another bit of movement caught her eye, and she followed it with her gaze. It looked like Elodie, still dressed all in black, but with the same determined stride she'd always had, walking toward the water on another part of the beach. Carolyn almost called out to her, but she knew the fog would muffle it. Maybe they'd have a chance to catch up tomorrow.

~

The girl at the counter at Harbor Fog the next morning looked too young to be working on a school day, and Elodie was nowhere to be seen.

"Is Elodie working today?" Carolyn asked after placing her order for the café's signature drink.

The girl glanced at a piece of paper tacked to the wall and shook her head. "Nope, day off."

"Weird question, but do you know if she's still living at her parents' house?"

The girl shrugged in response.

"Okay, thanks. Um, Wi-Fi working today?"

"Nope, still waiting on the tech."

"Great. Then to go. Which I guess I already told you."

The girl nodded and retreated to make Carolyn's drink.

Carolyn perused the small bulletin board above the table with cream and sugar available for patrons. It was business cards for housecleaning services and junk removal, flyers for the area's small churches, and a note about a memorial service for Tony, which wasn't scheduled until after she planned to head back to Seattle. Well, she could pick up a card once she was back in the city and mail that to Mrs. Dawson.

Her drink ready, Carolyn headed back to the rental house to work, but her attention kept being pulled away from her laptop and toward the weird driftwood mask. Somehow, every time she looked at it, she remembered watching Elodie striding onto the misty beach like a woman on a mission. Carolyn couldn't fathom what her former best friend might have been doing. They'd lost touch, and she didn't know what Elodie was into these days. Maybe standing on a mist-shrouded beach was her nightly meditation. Maybe she, too, had heard the football players and also wanted them to keep it down.

Carolyn shrugged and tried to get back to her work.

After the fifth time she found herself staring at the mask, she saved her document, marched over to the mask, and carried it to the spare bedroom, closing the door behind her.

Then she got back to work.

~

Carolyn was a little surprised by how much she stumbled up the steps of the rental house. She hadn't had *that* much to drink at the Seaside. Or maybe she had. Fish and chips hadn't been appealing, so she'd picked at an order of fries. And now that she counted the drinks people had bought for her, maybe it *had* been a lot.

But what else was she supposed to do, under constant grilling about how she'd been and was she happy to be back and had she ever thought about coming back for good (the answers to which had progressed from "great," "you bet," and "not really" to "fine," "I guess," and "no" as the evening wore on)? It was like all her classmates had kept up with one another so much that she was the only one of interest, so everyone had wanted to talk to her.

And Elodie hadn't been there, so she hadn't been able to get any snarky commentary on the lives of her former classmates. Especially the way several of them said "You always get called back to the sea," like it was some unofficial school motto or something.

She slumped onto the couch, where she'd left an unopened bottle of water, knowing she'd need it when she returned. As she cracked the seal and started guzzling it, she stared vacantly across the small living room.

Right into the eyes of the creepy driftwood mask.

She frowned, her eyes narrowing. She'd put it in the spare bedroom. She was sure of it. What was it doing back out here?

Her gaze swept across the room. Had Mrs. Dawson or maybe Bonnie come by to tidy things up? It didn't seem like it, seeing as the sweatshirt she'd worn to the coffee shop earlier was still balled up on the recliner and the boots she'd thought about wearing to the bar were still discarded in the middle of the living room floor. No one could have put the mask back on the end table without encountering her boots, at the very least.

She swallowed another gulp of water before rising unsteadily from the couch. Grabbing the mask, she opened the spare bedroom door and tossed the mask onto the bed.

As she closed the door a second time, she mumbled, "And stay there."

~

Carolyn woke to something scraping her leg, which was not a good accompaniment to her throbbing head and mouth like sandpaper. She pushed it out of her mind long enough to open the bottle of water she'd left on the bedside table and swallow the ibuprofen with a big gulp. Her mouth then feeling more human, and with the knowledge her headache would be departing, she tossed back the sheet and blanket to look at her leg.

There, on the fitted sheet, sat the driftwood mask. And where it had been pressed against her leg remained a crust of dried saltwater.

"What the fuck?" Carolyn asked aloud. She'd closed and locked the windows before she went out. She'd put the mask away, again. She'd locked the doors, even in her drunken state. There was no possible way the mask could be in her bed.

And yet, there it was, looking at her with asymmetric eye holes.

She marched into the kitchen, grabbed the largest plastic container and lid she found, and threw the mask into it. Once sealed, she carried it into the spare room yet again, put it inside the closet, and stacked several volumes of the long out-of-date encyclopedia set atop it.

"Stay," she intoned.

Closing the door behind her, she checked the time. She had several hours to get ready before the official reunion. She wished she'd asked Elodie for her number when she'd seen her at the coffee shop—it would be nice to have someone to talk to while they got ready together, the way they used to in high school. She still remembered Elodie's parents' number, but she wasn't sure she wanted to make small talk with them to get ahold of Elodie.

For a minute, she even considered heading back to Seattle and skipping the reunion. But she talked herself out of that. She was sure she'd have fun at the reunion, despite all the weirdness of being back after so long. Anyway, she hadn't spent $300 on a new dress for nothing.

~

Carolyn pulled her lacy black domino mask into place as she climbed the stairs to the high school gymnasium. She found it ironic that a class reunion, where people had often changed dramatically from their high school appearances, was also a masked ball. How they were going to recognize each other, she had no idea.

What she didn't expect was walking into the gym and being confronted with a crowd of people in suits and dresses, but all wearing driftwood masks like the one in her rental. Their asymmetrical faces turned toward her in unison, all blank expressions with their eyes hidden in shadow.

Someone took Carolyn's hand. She looked down at it and recognized Elodie's collection of eclectic silver rings. She'd been ready to jerk away, but now she squeezed Elodie's hand, thankful for the reassurance.

"We're so glad you came back, Carolyn," Elodie said. But her voice was strange, burbling, like her mouth and throat were full of water.

"You always get called back to the sea," the others intoned, in unison.

Carolyn trembled, cold sweat breaking out across her body. Things had been weird in the bar when people had used that phrase separately. Now, as one, the creepiness factor shot through the roof.

She tried to free her hand from Elodie's, but her best friend kept a tight grasp on her.

"Don't go, Carolyn," Elodie said. "We've missed you. Isn't it nice to be home?"

Again, the others spoke together. "You always get called back to the sea."

"No, no it is not," Carolyn said. "It's creepy and I don't know what's going on!"

"You'll understand," Elodie replied, leading Carolyn deeper into the gym. "Let's just find you a different mask."

Carolyn dug in her heels.

Elodie's grasp grew tighter, like a manacle enclosing Carolyn's hand.

Carolyn willed her hand to go limp, hoping it would slip out of Elodie's if she wasn't resisting, but to no avail. She let her entire body go limp next, trying to become dead weight.

But Elodie continued forward. And now Carolyn was surrounded by her former classmates, who seemed to buoy her along in Elodie's wake.

Reaching a table near the center of the gym with a display of dozens of driftwood masks, Elodie looked them over, still hauling Carolyn along behind her. "Which one? Which one?" she murmured before seizing a mask. She presented it to Carolyn. "Would you like to do the honors?"

"No, I would not!" Carolyn screamed. "I don't want to be here. I thought this would be fun, seeing you all again, but you've all turned into a cult or something. I just want to go home."

"You are home, Carolyn," Scott said from beside her, one of the crowd moving her along.

"You always get called back to the sea," the rest of her former classmates replied.

Elodie handed the mask to Scott, still maintaining her iron grip on Carolyn's hand. "Just put it on her."

Carolyn screamed, but that didn't stop Scott from slipping off her domino mask and replacing it with the driftwood mask.

And then, it was silent, her scream tamped down, drowned out by the roar of the sea within the wood as it adhered itself to her face.

Then she knew.

You can never really leave.

You always get called back to the sea.

PROGRESS

Some people say the mall is haunted, but most of those people don't know just how right they are. She's not a ghost, though, just an unclassifiable being. She lives in the hidden spaces in the underbelly of the beast, and she consumes peoples' dreams.

She's never gone hungry. From the time the mall was conceived, there have always been dreams in abundance. She was young then, her appetite not yet voracious, and she only took small nibbles from big dreams. It meant the architects didn't bother extending the decorative elements all the way to the third story. No one would really see them up there anyway, so why bother? It was a cost-saving measure, and they patted each other on the back at their cleverness.

And the architect who took a swan dive off the third-story railing into the majestic fountain in the center of the mall the day after they turned on the water to the fountain wasn't a huge surprise. He drank too much, his wife was unhappy with him, he was on the verge of getting fired.

It certainly couldn't have been because she gorged on one man's dreams, not realizing yet what that might do to a person. When his dreams were gone, what more did he have to live for?

She learned after that to choose dreams more cautiously, to skim just from the surface, not to slide her soda fountain straw all the way to the bottom of the glass and slurp up the last drops. The appliance salesmen with their eyes on a shiny new car made do with last year's model, saving the extra expense for a rainy day, or maybe blowing it on some other treat for themselves. The perfume counter girls with dreams of college found themselves content to turn on, tune in, drop out. Gone were their plans for marrying the men of their dreams, and instead they'd settle for those long-haired hippies who their parents told them had no future.

Maybe they didn't have a future either.

As the economy boomed, so too did the dreams. The shops filled the mall, in turn filled with customers, in turn filled with consumer culture and must-haves and big dreams of that perfect house, keeping up with the Joneses, and all that nonsense. The younger set came through too, their dreams perhaps not as ambitious yet, but all the more delicious for their fervent need for popularity and love, the adoration of their classmates, of being the coolest dudes and dudettes.

In those years, the dreams were so plentiful that even with only nibbles from each, she was full to bursting, and few of her victims even noticed what she'd taken from them, so full to bursting were they as well.

It was only when business started to dry up that she realized she'd grown too accustomed to a buffet of choices, and now she was dining on little more than crumbs.

The mall's fortunes waxed and waned, sometimes surging with the latest shops and trends, and people flocking to their doors to reclaim the nostalgia of youth, to knock out all the holiday shopping in one fell swoop, to wine and dine and shop till they dropped.

And drop they did, sometimes like flies, the store employees who were sure they'd get that next promotion if only they showed their devotion to their store, their brand, their look, their lifestyle. The early morning walkers, chasing the dream of eternal life through health and wellness, but forgetting that you can't outrun age and death, no matter how fit you become.

The mall gained its reputation as a haunted place then, the more dreamers she consumed beyond their capacity to bounce back. The crowds thinned, leaving her fewer choices than to prey upon the ones who were there, creating an alarming spate of mall security guards who clocked out, drove home, and left the car running in the garage until it ran out of gas and their families found them, still in the driver's seat, but no longer there.

Before too long, the shops thinned out, too. No one wants to shop at a haunted mall, especially not one with every other shop window papered or painted over, blacked out like dozens of missing teeth in a misshapen mouth.

Anyway, you could get everything you needed online. So why bother to set foot in a place with so few options, and no dreams left?

She might have starved herself out of existence if it wasn't for the little things that came and went, the pop-up holiday shops and haunted houses in the storefronts, and special events and mega-churches in the theaters. But the pickings were slim, the nourishment sporadic, and soon it dwindled down to nothingness.

Then came the clattering, the shattering of glass, the rending and tearing of steel, the disappearance of her secret places where she'd hidden away for decades. She found herself cast out, scrabbling across a cracked and weathered parking lot, until they ripped that up too, in the name of progress.

But progress was another sort of dream, and she lurked nearby, watching as her old home became a new home, a sprawling complex of shops and restaurants, topped with housing, glamourous and chic and state-of-the-art. She slipped herself into the spaces in the walls, felt the hum of electricity again.

And there, she found a surprise, data that surpassed anything she had ever felt in the old mall. And what's more, all that data was laden with dreams just out there for the harvesting, spewed across the digital landscape like an ornate fountain glutted with loose change from the wishes and dreams that passersby tossed in.

It was a firehose of sustenance, and she couldn't turn it off or stop letting it fill her out, fill her up, and expand her reach to so much more than she'd ever dreamed.

She doesn't need the so-called "new urban center," even with all the dreams it could provide. She's tapped into the world wide web, and she sits like a spider in the center, gobbling up the hopes and dreams borne aloft by this new commercial monstrosity, vaster than any mall she'd ever dreamed.

And finally, she is sated.

AUTUMN DAYS AND AUTUMN NIGHTS

The sun beats down, unseasonably warm for this time of year. Funeral cards become the fans of the moment, fluttering feebly, producing little relief. People unaccustomed to the dark uniform of the bereaved waver as their backs grow warm and their faces grow red and sweaty.

I'm cool as always, tucked in the shade of a towering elm, watching the proceedings, but never taking part.

How many of these funeral-goers wish they were not here, not because they regret the death of their loved one or friend, but because they never really cared for the deceased in the way they now claim?

My time is later, after these so-called mourners have departed.

I will care for those who have passed.

~

The rain pounds against my umbrella, hammering it into my clenched fist. Even in solid leather boots, the cold and damp seeps into my socks. The ground beneath is sodden, clumps of mud impossible to hide where heels and hard-soled shoes have churned the sod.

Lightning flashes, illuminating the dreary graveyard. The mourners have already rushed back to stately black cars. Their headlights illuminate the driving rain.

They drive away, perhaps to reminisce, but mostly to forget. Now or tomorrow or next year, all they want is to forget.

I will remember those who have passed.

~

Tonight, the air is crisp, tinged with the unmistakable scent of wood smoke in the distance. The leaves rustle beneath my gait, quick but shuffling, as I resist the urge to crunch through them like a child. There will be time for that later.

Now is when I focus on my goal.

The witching hour, the time when souls are split between light and dark, good and evil.

Or so they say.

The only quality of souls that concerns me is their ability to create an animating force.

Or, in my case, a re-animating force.

I do not judge.

Regardless of the state of their soul, I will love those who have passed.

~

I haunt the cemeteries nightly. Most nights, I am alone.

This night is different. It is dark and bears a chill breeze, but the families huddled together, with the light of candles and sipping chocolate, remain warm. Their voices ring with memories, stories shared, told time and again.

They mourn. They care. They remember.

The souls of their departed are vibrant with the knowledge they are still loved.

This is not my place to be, nor my souls to take. But I linger, awash in the feelings, so different from those to which I am accustomed.

This is my favorite night of fall.

Perhaps my favorite night of all.

~

Frost rimes the grass, the leaves, the stones, the trees. The cold seeps into my bones, chilling me to my core. Breath escapes my lips in a white cloud.

Not so that of my companions.

I raise them, in the sweltering heat, in the rain, in the chill, all through the autumn months. I bend them to my bidding. They follow me unwaveringly.

They are no longer flesh and bone, their mortal remains in various states of decay. But they are cared for. They are remembered. They are loved.

They are mine.

THE GRAVEYARD

The graveyard was choked with weeds, glitching Greg's camera with bursts of static. Something scurried in the underbrush, but nothing was visible.

"It's a mess," he said. "Shoulda brought a weedwhacker."

Melody shook her head. "Buncha cowards." She crouched, sighting across the weeds for the few tombstones poking above them, until she picked out the tallest. "There."

And then she was gone, whisked into the weeds by the scurrying things, whatever they were.

The rest didn't stick around to find out.

They just found bones deposited on their porches until all of Melody's skeleton was reunited with her erstwhile friends.

"The Graveyard" originally appeared in *Hawthorne and Ash*, January 2025.

WISH YOU WERE SLAIN

(Golden Shovel of "Wish You Were Gay" by Billie Eilish)

When it's down to just you and I,
you're gonna try to make me Laugh,
and maybe I will play Along,
but my heart won't be in it, Like
the spark has gone out and Nothing's
replaced it. You won't know what's Wrong,

you'll take my hand, and about Four
steps, before you realize Days
have passed, and your momentum Has
died. And behind you, you Never
noticed the killer's breathing Felt
so close. Cause I'm them now. So Long.

IF DEATH IS BUT THE KEY

If death is but the key,
what will it open?
If it is a door,
where will it lead?

If the key is a button,
what happens when it's pressed?
If we press it enough,
what will it change?

If the key brings insight,
what will it tell us?
If we are enlightened,
what will it mean?

If the key is a tone,
what will it sound like?
If we hear it,
what will we sing?

If death is but the key,
how can anything be unimportant?

THE VOID STARES BACK

I see you.
You stare into the distance,
contemplating the meaning of everything.
You conclude life is meaningless.
You sigh.

Your sighs crack
the bars of my prison.

I hear you.
No longer content to merely think
about your life and its meaning,
you tell your friends.
"I don't understand
why we keep pretending
things will get better.
We're all doomed."

Your despair opens the doors
between my world and yours.

I smell you.
After too many drinks,
too many cigarettes,
too many, too much,
anything to numb the emptiness.

I inhale it all,
filling my lungs with life.

I taste you.
When you shiver,
when you say someone's
walked over your grave,
it's not walking at all,

it's my tongue,
flickering through the barriers,
creeping up your spine.

I feel you.
I try you on
like a tailored suit,
no longer held back
by the barriers,
your despair
welcoming me
into a new home.

I become you.

MUSINGS ON THE PAST

(Waltmarie)

They say the past is dead and
buried,
but there's always someone trying to keep it
alive.
Will you let yourself continue to be
haunted,
as though his presence is
ceaseless,
or will you shake off the fear wrought
by him?

HOLLOW

The world never ends conveniently.

No, it ends when you're on a camping trip, trying to get away from your last failed relationship ("It's not you, it's me."), your poor job performance review ("Lacks attention to detail and focus."), or your nagging parents ("We won't be young forever."). Or all three.

And you're in a remote enough part of the countryside, with no cellular signal, that the only way you realize it's the end of the world is how blisteringly quiet it is. No distant planes, trains, or automobiles. Just silence.

Until you hear the baby wailing.

You've never been entirely sure what you should do when a baby cries. You usually settle for handing them back to their mum or dad and letting them deal with the problem.

But you haven't a clue what sort of apocalypse this is, whether it's taken some people but not all, or if you and this baby are the only people left alive.

At any rate, you're probably the only people for miles.

The problem with this weird little patch of countryside is it's nearly always foggy, which was a selling point when you chose it for camping (on account of it being so delightfully mysterious), but it makes tracking the direction the crying is coming from a bit of a challenge.

So you wander this way for a while, with the cries getting no nearer, then try another direction, and before long, you've lost sight of the bright crimson of your tent, and you're jumping at every eddy in the fog.

And at the sleek black cat that appears out of nowhere and meows, very much like a baby's cry.

But the baby's still crying, somewhere else. And the cat isn't about to help you find them.

You wonder if the baby is even within miles, or if there's just some weird quirk of the landscape that makes it seem closer.

But you can't ignore it, either. You'll go mad if you do.

So you keep searching.

One protein bar and half your canteen down, you spot something yellow in the mist. It's the only spot of color you've seen in hours (even your clothes seem to have lost their color to the dismal grey), so you light on it like a beacon.

But there's no baby there, only a discarded yellow quilt. Compared to the air around you, it's warm, as though it was just abandoned, still faintly scented like baby powder and lavender.

You bring it along so when you find the baby, you can reunite them with their blanket.

After all, they're still out there, still crying.

You keep searching. You lose track of time, but the sun hasn't set, nor does it give any indication it will be soon. Maybe that's just an effect of the fog. Or maybe that's the apocalypse *du jour*. At any rate, your canteen is empty, you've devoured all your protein bars, and your legs are burning from the exertion.

Maybe you should take a break, give your legs a rest, and regroup.

When you wake, your head is just as foggy as the moors around you. It's quiet. Has the baby stopped crying? You strain your hearing, certain there should be something.

But there's nothing. Just the silence, eerie now that there's nothing at all to hear.

You're not sure this is where you sat down for your rest. You thought you'd found a clearing, but now the trees are thick around you. Your canteen hangs from a low branch on one of them, thumping gently against the trunk as though full. Didn't you drain it before your rest? Didn't you use it as a pillow?

No, that must have been another day, another hike. Because it's full, and the water tastes crisp like it's just been refilled. And your knapsack (that's what you must have used for a pillow) has jerky and dried fruit. You don't recall seeing this brand before, but perhaps you grabbed it when your usual brand was sold out.

And still, the baby isn't crying. But you're certain they must be out there. You have their quilt, after all. You need to reunite it with the baby.

So you set out again, full canteen, full knapsack, and a small yellow quilt, wound around your arms, still smelling faintly of this baby you've never seen.

It's the first horn that blares as a car swerves around you that tells you you've made your way back to civilization, and your imagined apocalypse was perhaps an effect of the isolation of your camping spot. (Camping? Why would you have been camping? The baby is lost!)

You stumble on the sure footing of the sidewalk, your legs and feet so accustomed to uneven terrain you've forgotten how to walk on a level surface. More cars stream past before one stops, the passenger asking if you're alright.

"Where is the baby?" you croak, your voice hoarse from disuse.

They look at the driver, then back at you.

"The baby," you repeat.

They shake their heads. They drive away.

You still can't hear the baby's cries, but you know you have to find them. (Her, you think. The baby is a girl, though you can't recall her name. But you remember her now, a dusting of fair hair, bright blue eyes, looking up at you, crying.)

Your pace quickens. She has to be somewhere. You have to find her. She is ... she is your baby?

The moors, she must be on the moors. And you trudge back to the rolling terrain, with rocks and brush underfoot, and you walk until you hear her cries again.

You are always searching.

That is the way your world ends.

QUEEN OF THE ROLLER DISCO

Rink's haunted. Everybody knows that. But she don't mean you any harm. You give the Queen her song and the floor to herself, and she'll leave the other customers alone. If you don't ... well, that's how we got the Queen in the first place.

It was the seventies, and disco was King. But the rink had two Princes, too: Keith and Bruce. Rivals, of course, because that's how these stories go. They both wanted to gain acclaim for their disco skating, which meant they each needed a partner.

And that's where the Queen came in. She was the undisputed women's disco skating champion. The other ladies couldn't hold a candle to her. She got onto the floor, and it was like time stopped, every gaze in the place glued to her for the length of a song. Her song.

The Princes both wanted to make it their song, too. So they tried to woo her. Keith plied her with gifts—flowers, jewelry, fancy new skates in ebony and topaz, fit for the Queen she was. Bruce tried flattery instead, lacking Keith's bottomless pockets. Both trying, both knowing she could only choose one.

And she gave each of them a fair shake on the floor, seeing who could best compliment her style, who was more willing to let her shine as their partner.

It might have been inevitable that she chose Bruce. Keith's gifts were nice, but they were only things. Bruce cared—maybe only superficially at first, but it grew into something real. And Keith wanted to be as flashy as the Queen, while Bruce was all too happy to play second fiddle.

Keith, unsurprisingly, did not take rejection well.

He paired up with one of the other ladies, but he knew they'd never reach the success the Queen and Bruce were destined for.

So Keith played dirty. Suddenly, the center of the floor, where the Queen and Bruce practiced their most intricate moves, was overly waxed and treacherous. Another night, the bearings in the Queen's gorgeous new skates failed spectacularly, locking up her wheels and shedding stray ball bearings, providing tripping hazards for Bruce.

But the final straw came when the Queen skated up to the booth to ask the DJ to spin her song, and he showed her the cracked record.

Her eyes blazed, and she turned her fury toward Keith. She called him out, her voice carrying in the silence between records.

"You ruined my song."

Keith's languid shrug and smirk only made it worse.

The Queen flew across the floor, her wheels consuming the distance, and shoved him.

Somehow, he didn't move.

But he shoved back.

The Queen's eyes were wide as she fell, arms pinwheeling. She was the best, but caught off guard, gravity kicked in.

Bruce had followed her, ready to deal with Keith himself.

At least until the Queen's head bounced off Bruce's skate.

The impact wasn't loud, but the implications of it were ear-shattering in the silent rink.

And the Queen wasn't moving.

She would never move again.

Everyone blamed Keith, but the judge and jury called it an accident, with no one to blame.

Still, Keith knew better than to ever show his face near the rink again.

As for Bruce, he spent more time in the rink bar than with his skates on. But he bought a new record of her song and handed it to the DJ. And every night, he asked the DJ to clear the floor and play her song, so he could skate his part and imagine the Queen was still in his arms.

The booze slowed him down, and eventually he stopped skating. The DJ still spun her song, but Bruce just ordered another drink while staring at the empty floor, as though he could only imagine the two of them skating there together.

And then, one night, Bruce wasn't there anymore either. Found out what happened to him from the unlucky bastard who came across Bruce's wrecked car, wrapped around a tree like embracing a lover, 8-track still playing the Queen's song.

A week later, once word had reached the regulars about Bruce's death, the DJ left the Queen's song out of the rotation. Out of respect for the dead, he said, both the Queen and Bruce.

And that's when the Queen raged. Her spirit, trapped in the rink, shrieked in the subconscious of every patron. Everyone on the floor and everyone in the bar, they all felt her pain, her wrath, and her need.

She would not—must not—be forgotten.

And that's when the tradition started. Give the Queen her song and let her have her skate. Once every night. More if you're feeling generous.

Don't forget.

She's no longer a benevolent Queen.

MODERN ISO ONNA

Manami had adapted, wearing modern styles, darker shades, fishnets, and heavy eyeliner. It seemed reasonable for a goth girl to be sitting atop a cliff, staring out toward the sea.

And it still brought in plenty of victims.

She encouraged the young men who saw her, looking over her shoulder and speaking quietly to lure them closer. By the time they reached her, they'd forgotten why they came, entranced by her voice and the sea, and walked straight off the cliff.

Then Manami, the iso onna, dove from the cliff and followed them beneath the waves to consume their blood.

"Modern Iso Onna" originally appeared in *Short Fantasy Stories*, July 2025.

GLAISTIG

Eimhir had always disliked her old-fashioned name, but she hadn't expected her name would tie her so closely to Scottish legends. Who murders a woman and stuffs them up a chimney, like the glaistig of yore?

Her boyfriend, apparently.

Ex-boyfriend, more accurately.

She also wasn't expecting him to move on so quickly. But there he was, with a new woman in tow.

Eimhir willed herself into the woman's phone. She shrieked "murderer," startling them both.

Thankfully, the woman understood the danger and immediately called the authorities.

Eimhir suspected she'd soon be free of her ex, as well as this world.

"Glaistig" originally appeared in *Hawthorne and Ash*, January 2025.

BY OMENS BOUND

Haunting the cemetery,
no ghost, but instead a crow,
black as the night's velvet embrace,
lurking in the dark,
watching the proceedings.

Living nearby, the local folk
say it's an omen, a harbinger,
with superstitions about
what its presence and
behavior mean.

Like when it caws three times
during a funeral,
it means it knows
a secret, still hidden,
about the deceased.

Or if it lands on someone's coffin,
the person it's nearest to
is the one responsible
for the events leading
to the dead's demise.

But when it flies down, mid-service,
and snatches the black gloves
from the widow's hands, and
flies off, the local folk can only
speculate about the meaning.

And speculate they will,
for years on end, at least
until it happens a second time,
and then they'll have two data points
to draw conclusions from.

But the crow doesn't know
secrets or truths, or even why
it took a woman's gloves.
It's just bound here, ever watching,
like a ghost who cannot leave.

THE BIRTHDAY PARTY

The table, set.
The vase, resplendent with blooms.
The cake, cut with precision.
The guests, assembled.

The person of the hour, missing.
But the party must go on.

The lots, drawn.
The honoree, selected.
The party, continued.
The fun, mandatory.

The (new) person of the hour, aged.
Someone has to be.

GAMBLING

They say the thaw won't come for weeks.
They prove it by putting things on the ice:
sticks, cardboard boxes, children's toys,
a rubber duckie, joined soon after by dozens more.

But one man thinks he can beat them all.
A car, he suggests, no engine or seats,
light as it can be without fully dismantling,
parked on the lake, at least until the thaw.

They've plenty of junkers to donate one,
and everyone places their bets on the thaw date.
He'll generously pass the funds on
to a charity of the winner's choosing.

But there's a secret,
hidden inside the rusted heap,
and he's gambling on
no one realizing the truth

before the car
  falls through the melting ice,
        contents never to be seen
again.

ROLLER COASTER

---

there's a void in the roller coaster
in the part where the tracks
run through a tunnel.
as long as you're
buckled in
you're safe.
well, at least safe
from falling into the void.
there's no way to control things
flying out of the void, landing
on the riders, or coating
them in the debris
from somewhere
not here.
so get ready
for the onslaught
of who knows what
from who knows where
and hold on for your life!

WAY OUT (SEND SELFIES)

Review article submission to MusicNews, 11/23/2022

Fans were shocked by the recent disappearance of the so-called King of Lyrical Realism, Oscar Toben. But some claim the song titles on Toben's latest album, *Way Out (Send Selfies)* (released 10/31/2022), suggest the album is a hidden message from Toben to his super fans.

Unfortunately, such claims have proven impossible to verify, as all who have posted such an assertion online have similarly gone missing. These fans, all over the world, have disappeared without a trace, just like their idol. Local authorities have found no leads on Toben or his fans.

This mystery has cast a pall over analysis of *WO(SS)*, but serious Lyrical Realism aficionados persist in deciphering the symbolism of the lyrics and their juxtaposition with Toben's previous oeuvre.

The album commences with "Across the Darkened Meadow," an instrumental except for a brief phrase spoken at the end: "Don't let them find you." Toben has largely eschewed instrumentals in the past, making his opening the album with this song an interesting choice.

The next three songs, "And Under the Lost Bower," "Dive Down Deep and Breathe to Cross," and "At the Other Side," share a common droning lullaby-esque melody, the simplicity of which could serve to allow their individual lyrics to shine. But strangely, Toben does not take advantage of this opportunity to its fullest effect. Instead, the bulk of the vocals are buried within the instrumentation. Attempts to separate the tracks revealed these vocals were recorded in the same track as the bassoon, which has baffled audiophiles.

The midpoint of the album is "If You Hear," which is listed as an acapella song, but the song's only words are those of the title, spoken and layered for a reverb effect that works for precisely the one minute, ten second, length of the song. A moment beyond that and it would be madness inducing.

With "Footsteps in the Forest," we finally receive what we expect from the King of Lyrical Realism himself, from the sparse drumbeat mimicking footfalls to the lyrics stating the drums or footsteps are not in the song itself, but rather they are following the listener through this forest soundscape. Toben's use of "they" in this context, particularly as related to the "them" in the opening and closing songs, heightens the sense of paranoia within the album.

Already "Only Read the Highs" is the subject of some confusion, and as his is way, Toben gave no indication as to which school of thought is correct in liner notes or interviews prior to his disappearance. That the song begins with the same footfalls from the previous song leads some to interpret the "highs" as the spaces between the footsteps, while the whisper-light chanting, a callback to the Gregorian chant trend of 1990, at the end of the song links this to the subsequent song.

Notably, however, "Etching Koine Italics," contains no notes higher than middle C, rendering the potential "highs" in this song rather low on the musical register. The Koine Greek lyrics of this song makes their interpretation out of reach to this reviewer, who is in pursuit of a translator and hopes to make an addendum to this review subsequently.

Finally, the album ends much as it began, with "No, Go" also an instrumental, with the sole and final words, "Don't let them forget you," in striking counterpoint to the opening lyrics.

~

KoLR Fan Gathering website

PosterChild (11/11/22, 17:05): I read Argentine's theory that if you take the first letter of each word of the song titles, it spells out a message. Sure, the last four songs are FITF ORTH EKI NG, "fit for the king".

But the first five don't make any sense. ADTM AUTLB DDDABTC ATOS IYH. Even taking out "the" (which you can't do in the final titles) doesn't make sense.

To me, the titles read more like directions.

Has anyone tried following them?

~

Oscar Toben's YouTube channel

Comment (AutoTranscript201):

December 1, 2022, video posted at 12:01 a.m.

The video begins with a black screen and the opening notes of "Across the Darkened Meadow," from Oscar Toben's *Way Out (Send Selfies).*

At the three-second mark, a selfie of Toben appears, showing his eyes and forehead only. His pupils are heavily dilated.

At the ten-second mark, a second selfie of Toben appears, this one showing only the lower half of his face. His smile is wide, open-mouthed, and something shines from beyond his teeth.

The video continues in similar rhythm, showing split selfies, two separate photos for upper and lower face of other individuals, each on screen for seven seconds, as the entirety of *Way Out (Send Selfies)* plays.

All photos share similarities to Toben's photo, with dilated pupils, open mouths, and something unidentifiable lurking behind their teeth.

No one has noses.

END TRANSCRIPT

720 comments deleted.

Comment (YouTubeModeration): Video removed.

Comment (KoLRHunter): This comment probably won't last long, so copypasta, friends. Get the word out.

Amsterdam police sent a warrant to YouTube offices to have this video removed when it was found that several of the people portrayed in selfies were missing persons from their jurisdiction, all of whom had disappeared after making posts on the KoLR Fan Gathering website.

Several fans had already downloaded the video to personal servers, leading to a thread of posts on the KoLR Fan Gathering website wherein each person pictured was identified as a missing fan.

While the video's metadata revealed the upload was genuinely from Oscar Toben's production company, no metadata remained for the images. The production company confirmed they couldn't locate the video or the images from which it was constructed on their servers. They allowed digital forensics investigators to confirm the absence of these files.

Fans have continued to vanish. Several have noted they plan to follow PosterChild's theory of the song titles as directions.

Any meadow will do as a starting point.

Don't know where it will lead me, but I'll see you on the flipside.

THE MAN BEHIND THE MOON

It's like one of those toys where you can turn the head around to change its expression. Only instead of happy and sad, the two faces are pockmarked or shadowed.

But the Man Behind the Moon isn't just another face. He's the moon's hype man. He reminds us the moon is the most important thing around, and we'd be lost without it.

Without the moon, he says, bad things will happen to the climate and oceans. And knowing the sort of *things* that live in the oceans, do you want to risk anything that could invoke their wrath?

He says without the moon, we would have to face the reality that Canada no longer exists. Only through the moon's grace does it remain in our memories, and thus lives on.

And what about the tunnel from the North to South Pole and the strange, violent beings who traverse it? The moon is Earth's only defense, casting its rays across each end of the tunnel to keep the beings in.

Nonsense, you say. Canada exists, and there's no tunnel through the Earth.

No? asks the Man Behind the Moon. Are you sure? Perhaps a few more words of praise to the moon (and his hype man) might be in order.

What harm could a few prayers do?

They certainly can keep the Man Behind the Moon's face from looming ever larger in your mind and your heart.

Just give him what he wants, and it will all be fine.

AURORA DOLFÓNOS

After the Northern Lights were visible much farther south than ever before, the questions started.

"But did you hear the angels?"

Most people hadn't. Those who had spoke of ethereal singing accompanying the shifting lights. And most of them agreed it could be nothing other than angels.

They didn't question why they continued to hear those songs on quiet nights without the Northern Lights. Nor did they question what the angels told them to do.

It was only when the murder cases made headlines that they settled upon pleas of "temporary insanity triggered by auditory hallucinations" as their only defense.

"Aurora Dolfónos" originally appeared in *Reach Your Apex*'s BlueSky feed, September 2025.

THE HOUSE

Hikaru knows the house wasn't here yesterday.

She hikes this trail daily with Bounder, so named for the way she bounds up the foothills east of Seattle when she's allowed off leash. Today, Bounder is still, staring at the house when Hikaru comes around the bend in the trail. She gazes up at Hikaru, ice blue eyes wide, and maybe a slight furrow of her forehead, evident only to the human who knows her better than anyone.

Hikaru checks her GPS. They haven't strayed from the trail. This is their regular route.

She texts her sister—habit, or ritual, checking in whenever she pauses mid-hike. Kimiko will already know—she monitors Hikaru's location on hikes, ever since she decided she couldn't keep up with Hikaru's relentless pace. It's the buddy system in the digital age.

The house isn't the sort of thing that could have been built overnight. It reminds Hikaru of the witch's house from Hansel and Gretel, an old Victorian with ornate white wooden trim like delicate icing, windows lightly glazed like sugar glass. It's not cold enough for frost, she thinks, though maybe at this elevation, at night, it is. That must be it. The sun just hasn't burned it off yet.

Her phone buzzes. "Text not sent."

Her signal's vanished. It's never been a problem on this trail before. There's just enough tech money in this area to ensure a proliferation of cell towers, even in what looks like wilderness.

Bounder whines. She knows they should continue.

"Just once around the house?" Hikaru asks.

Bounder lays down, her opinion clear. Hikaru can do what she wants. Bounder sticks to the trail.

Hikaru snaps a photo with her phone. "Evidence." Then she leaves Bounder behind as she skirts around the house, taking more photos as she goes.

There's a point, just before she reaches the back of the house, where she can still look back and see Bounder. The dog's gaze is fixed on Hikaru. They both know that when Hikaru takes one more step, she'll be out of view.

It's a sound that does it. Just a quiet exhalation, like a tiny sigh. It's not Hikaru, and it's not Bounder. There's someone else.

Hikaru plunges forward, toward a back door just barely ajar.

~

Kimiko and the search and rescue team arrive at the clearing by mid-afternoon. Bounder hasn't moved an inch, but she whines when she sees a familiar face.

Kimiko scratches behind Bounder's ears, trying to soothe her sister's dog. "Where'd she go, girl?"

Bounder's gaze returns to the clearing, flat and empty.

Kimiko turns to the young man heading up the search and rescue team—Bradley. "This is the last place I got a signal from her phone. But she'd never willingly leave Bounder behind."

He nods. "Spread out, guys. Ma'am, wait here with her dog, please."

Kimiko doesn't enjoy being called "ma'am," but she does as she's asked.

~

It doesn't make sense, but Hikaru thinks the house feels content. Maybe she's projecting. The house is warm and comfortable, with overstuffed furniture you can sink right into. The kitchen smells like fresh-baked cookies. It's cozy, not sterile and utilitarian, like Hikaru's tiny apartment. It's the sort of place she'd love to live, away from the bustle of the city, hiking right at her doorstep. If only she'd brought Bounder with her, she'd never need to leave.

As things are, though, Bounder isn't here. And Hikaru can't find a door to go back out to get her.

She notices motion outside and sees her sister standing beside Bounder. She waves but gets no response.

If only her phone had a signal, she'd text Kimiko and invite her in too, at least to visit.

~

"Sorry, ma'am, there's no trace of your sister nearby," Bradley says. "We'll keep looking, but you should go on home."

Kimiko looks up from her phone, where she's still trying to track Hikaru's phone to no avail. She, at least, has a signal here.

Bounder still hasn't moved, even when Kimiko offered her favorite treats. Kimiko brought a spare leash, too, but she's not looking forward to trying to haul a recalcitrant Husky away from the spot to which she's rooted herself.

"C'mon, Bounder," she says. "We'll come back tomorrow."

Bounder gazes up at Kimiko, her forehead still wrinkled with concern. But she rises all the same, lets Kimiko clip the leash to her collar, and follows her second-favorite human.

As they turn away from the clearing, Kimiko can't remember why she and Bounder went hiking so late. She checks the time on her phone. Nearly six. They've stayed out far longer than she thought they would. She looks down at Bounder. "Wanna jog, girl?"

Bounder's tongue lolls from her mouth. She can't remember why she was here, either. But it will be good to run and go home and snuggle on the couch with her favorite human.

~

Inside the house, Hikaru can only watch and sob.

BLACK, WHITE, GRAY, ORANGE

It had taken an hour to get the generator running in the pitch black of the yard, but now that it was, the gentle hum of functional electricity was luring Mara and Keith to sleep. Gone were their worries about getting out of the city or running out of gas on the way. No one had stayed at her family's vacation home in at least six months, but the solar cells retained enough energy to power all 5,000 square feet.

"Told you my dad was one step off from a prepper," Mara murmured drowsily.

"Does that mean we'll be eating beans and canned peaches until this whole thing blows over?" Keith asked.

"Probably."

Keith rolled over beside her, rustling the ridiculously high thread-count sheets in the main suite.

The rustling continued, even after he'd stopped moving.

"Do you hear that?" Mara asked.

Keith didn't respond, other than the faint, slow breathing of sleep. Ever since they'd met, that had been his superpower—falling asleep and staying that way until morning.

She lay still, listening in the darkness. It wasn't trees in the wind or the surf. She knew those sounds from countless vacations. With all the windows closed, nature was impossible to hear.

Whatever this was had to be much, much closer.

She slipped out from under the covers, thankful they'd been able to charge their phones on the drive up. She shone the flashlight around, its beam illuminating the tasteful whites and grays of the main suite. She checked under the bed and in the bathroom and closets for some critter that had somehow managed to get into the locked house.

Nothing.

But the noise was still there.

Mara stopped in the hallway, trying to determine the direction over her heart beating loudly in her ears.

It sounded like it was inside the walls.

But that didn't make sense either. Even though no one had *stayed* in the house for six months, that didn't mean no one had been here. There were cleaners and groundskeepers who lived nearby and kept the place up during the off-season. If there'd been any sort of maintenance problem that afforded egress into the house, they'd have taken care of it.

But that didn't change the fact that *something* was making noise.

Unbidden, a memory of her aunt's house came to her. It had been an older, two-story house, with laundry chutes in two of the bathrooms on the upper and lower floors. When people went in or out the front door, the metal laundry chute doors clattered.

This house didn't have laundry chutes, but it did have a central vacuum cleaner system. The inlet covers were spring-loaded to snap shut when they weren't in use. They shouldn't rattle. Or rustle.

One of the inlets was in the hallway, just outside the main suite. Mara crouched to put her ear at the same level.

It was definitely the source of the rustling.

There wasn't an inlet in the main suite. Her mother had insisted on that. Mara scrambled back into the bedroom, closing the door behind her.

She scooted a recliner in front of the door, just to make sure nothing was getting in.

~

Keith shook Mara's shoulder to wake her. "Hon, why is the recliner in front of the door?"

Bleary-eyed, Mara recounted the sound she'd heard after he fell asleep, and where she'd determined it was coming from.

Laughing lightly, he said, "You told me this place is locked up tighter than Fort Knox. Plus, those tubes are what, a couple of inches in diameter?"

"I know. Maybe it's some paper or something that got stuck in there, and the system keeps trying to pull it in. But in the middle of the night, in the dark, and with everything going on back home ... better safe than sorry, right?"

"Sure. The system's got a receptacle or whatever in the basement, right? And that's probably where we're going to find out how many varieties of beans we have on hand?"

She nodded.

"Then let's go down there and see if we can hear it running." He paused, listening. "Or maybe it finally got whatever it was unstuck."

"Yeah, I don't hear it either. Shower first, or do we want to see if there's coffee?"

He looked toward the bedroom door, then toward the bathroom. "Tough choice."

Feeling emboldened in the light of morning, Mara said, "You go ahead. I'll go look for coffee."

He leaned across the bed to kiss her. "Best girlfriend."

Mara slipped on a robe from her parent's closet, then scooted the chair out of the way of the bedroom door.

She was in the basement pantry when she heard the rustle again, louder and closer.

The single bulb overhead flickered.

The pantry occupied a utility space in the basement, with pipes and wiring exposed across the ceiling. The white PVC tubing was part of the vacuum system, she thought. Her gaze traced several branches of that tubing to a dark corner of the utility room, where the central receptacle was attached, about halfway up the wall.

With fumbling hands, she shone her phone's flashlight into the corner. A black spot, with jagged edges, marred the exterior of the white receptacle, a streak of gray trailing from it.

No, that wasn't a spot. That was a hole. The streak was dust and debris.

And the two orange glowing points in the darkness of the hole mirrored the ones people saw before everything went pear-shaped, before people started being attacked and killed by some sort of creature.

She didn't have time to scream before she joined their number.

MONSTER UNDER MY BED

There's a monster under my bed. She looks exactly like me. She doesn't scare me, like some monsters. We're friends.

Sometimes, we swap places. She doesn't believe in bedtimes, so she stays up reading books in my bed. Sometimes, she reads them aloud, and I help her with words she doesn't know.

She says she won't always be here, because someday I'll grow up and decide monsters aren't real. I tell her that will never happen, because I want her to be my friend forever.

So far, I'm winning. Under the bed is the perfect place to trap a monster.

"Monster Under My Bed" originally appeared in *Reach Your Apex*'s BlueSky feed, October 2025.

THE EYES ARE ALWAYS WATCHING

I catch my nephew, Colin, the budding mad scientist, pouring his green "fruit" drink into his school science project, trying to sprout a potato from the eyes.

"What are you doing?"

"I wanna see what'll happen."

This seems like a "my parents are away, so auntie will let me do whatever" ploy. But I have zero investment in this science experiment's success or failure.

I play along. "What's your hypothesis?"

"I wanna grow a green-eyed potato, so I'm giving it green juice."

"Okay, I guess we'll see what happens."

He nods cheerily.

~

By dinner, the potato's taken on some of the dye from the "juice".

"Hey, it's turning green," I say.

He frowns. "Not green-eyed, though."

I'm not sure what he means, but I try to encourage him. "Growing things takes time, right?"

"Yes, but I need to show my project next Friday."

"Then you've got ten days."

His shoulders slump, but he nods.

I add "green drink" to the grocery list.

~

Despite the green drink's sugar content, two nights later, the potato has a several-inch-long sprout.

Colin pours more into the jar before bedtime.

I'm finishing up the dishes after reading him a story, and I notice the water in the jar is clear, the green leached out.

The sprout's doubled in length.

There's a bud at the end, like it's trying to push forth a new potato in midair.

Then the bud opens, a glowing green eye, human-like, in its center.

What is in that juice?

JRRRR THE SUMMONER

My gaming group tells me magic isn't real when I start writing spells in a language I invented. Brad says I'm a Tolkien wannabe. The others laugh and start calling me "Jrrrr."

Jrrrr's a decent name for a wizard.

I keep working on my spells. They stop reminding me what days we're going to game.

I don't mind. I learned enough from the game books.

And the ones from the occult store.

I run into the gaming group after school one day, but I'm ready.

They're not, when I summon a literal hellhound to drag them out of my life.

"Jrrrr the Summoner" originally appeared in *Short Fantasy Stories*, July 2025.

THE DROP GETS YOU EVERY TIME

Is it the taut extent
of a hangman's noose,
(if you're lucky)
a measured drop?

Is it the feeling of falling
when you're drifting to sleep,
only this time
you really drop?

Or is it when you're tossed
into an oubliette,
just waiting, forgotten,
an angstloch drop?

INVASIVE

Creeping, tentative,
closer to the corpse.
Probing, searching,
looking for the right nutrients.
Digging, infiltrating,
sucking out the marrow.

Wrapping, shifting,
lifting the old bones,
still in pristine order,
not a one misplaced.
Combining one spark of life
with the magic still there.

Moving now, searching,
wanting to take flight,
but knowing the ivy leaves
can't support the weight
of the skeletal dragon
they've invaded and revived.

WOOD WIDE WEB

Deep as the roots go,
intertwined with hyphae,
in a strange sort of symbiosis
with messages whizzing
across the mycorrhizal network
like plant-based emails.

It's part mutual aid
and part social network
and just the thing
for planning action
right beneath the noses
of their oppressors.

With the news of development
breaking on the wood wide web,
the trees prepare a united front
crowding at the edges of the forest,
impenetrable, a thickset thicket,
dense and massive.

And their scouts and runners,
the fungi, their eyes and ears,
in a manner of speaking,
hard to root out
when they're all underground
and evade the shovel's sting.

And even as winter falls,

and the trees disrobe,
the fungal heart beats on,
untouched by the frost,
and spreading the word
across the subterranean.

SOMETHING IN THE WATER

There's something in the water,
and it's definitely not safe.

Only takes a teaspoon
to drown a person,
and there's much more
than a teaspoon
in rivers and lakes.

Or maybe it's filled
with alkalines,
which may or may not
be sufficient
to saponify your fat.

Or if you do drown,
you might be food
for fish and other critters,
not that you'd really care
at that point.

Or maybe it's merfolk,
not unlike the fae,
who don't want you dead.
You're much more useful
to them alive.

It's definitely not safe,
because there's something in the water.

LOST LAGOON

"How long is this lagoon cruise supposed to be?" Simon asked, checking the time on his phone.

"Just under an hour, I think," Gabrielle replied. "But lagoon is wrong. It's a lake. We're nowhere near the ocean, and there's no water flow in or out of this place."

"Right. We've been on the boat for an hour and a quarter, though."

Gabrielle frowned. "Well, it must be close to done, then." She leaned across Simon to peer out the window. "Huh, that's weird. You'd think we'd be coming up on the dock by now."

"Yeah. I'd suggest we go out on deck, so we can be ready to go when we get to the dock, but it's hotter than hell out there."

"It's not the heat—" Gabrielle began.

Simon joined in for the second part. "—it's the humidity." It was what all their college friends who had converged on Florida in July for Jules and Max's wedding kept saying. And it wasn't entirely wrong. The forecast only called for a high of eighty-five. But the humidity was nearly one hundred percent, and being outside of air-conditioned spaces was torturous for those more accustomed to northern climates, like Simon and Gabrielle were.

Simon pointed out the window. "Hang on, those trees over there. Do they look familiar to you?

~

The boat pitched, and Gabrielle clasped her hands over her stomach. "Oh my God, I drank too much last night for this."

"Just a little turbulence, babe." Simon wrapped an arm around her shoulders. "It'll settle out soon."

Gabrielle squeezed her eyes shut, but it made the boat's motion feel worse, her stomach queasier. She forced herself to stare at the shoreline, tricking her brain into thinking she and the boat were as stable and level as the terrain at the edge of the lake.

A stand of half a dozen trees, arranged in a circle around a wide stump, caught her attention.

~

"Yeah, we passed those trees before," Gabrielle said. "When the turbulence started earlier."

None of the other passengers seemed to notice the lake cruise had been going on longer than anticipated. They were engrossed with their phones or conversations or stared out the windows and watched the scenery go by. A few braved the deck, mostly those with enormous telephoto lenses on their cameras, shooting pictures of wildlife.

Toward the back of the cabin, a young woman wearing the nautical-themed uniform of the lake cruise leaned against the wall, reading a paperback novel with a spine so worn she held it in one hand, the pages she'd already read wrapping around to obscure the book's cover.

Gabrielle approached her and read her nametag. "Excuse me, Trina. Do you know how much longer we'll be cruising today?"

Trina didn't look up from her book. "Cruise is about fifty minutes."

"Right, that's what the brochure said, but it's quarter past now. We started an hour and fifteen minutes ago."

Holding a finger in the book to mark her spot, Trina fished her phone from her pocket. "Huh, well, we should have started out on the hour, but we must have gotten a late start." She glanced toward the shoreline and frowned, then approached the windows on the left side of the boat, nearest the shore. "That's weird."

"What's weird?" Gabrielle asked.

"The tiny little stream over there. It doesn't connect to anything, but it's one of the landmarks on the cruise—"

~

A crunch and a grinding sound beneath the boat interrupted Simon and Gabrielle's discussion of whether they should try to get their friend Frankie to dance with one of Max's cousins or siblings at the reception.

"Boats aren't supposed to make that sort of noise, are they?" Gabrielle asked.

Simon shrugged. "Sounds like when I learned how to drive a stick-shift. Maybe we've got a trainee captain or something."

"Are they called captains when they're still in training?"

"No idea." He glanced out the window. "But we're still moving. I'm sure it's fine.

~

"—We shouldn't be anywhere near there right now."

"Are we making a second circuit of the lake?" Gabrielle asked.

Trina shook her head. "We almost never do a double circuit. I'll look into it." She opened a door marked "Staff Only" but didn't close it behind her.

Gabrielle glanced back at Simon, who was looking at something on his phone, then followed Trina through the door and up the stairs.

"Hey, Case," Trina said. "We're not doing a double today, are we?"

The voice that replied was terse, stiff. "No."

"We just passed the streambed."

"Yeah, I know."

"But not doing a double."

A long sigh. "I missed the dock."

Gabrielle bit back a gasp. *What the hell?*

Trina seemed to share her disbelief. "Missed the dock? How?"

"I didn't see it."

"That's impossible. It's got people in ridiculous outfits swinging bright yellow rope—"

~

The dock loomed ahead, two attendants in nautical-themed uniforms waving as they readied the bright yellow ropes that held the ship against the dock.

Gabrielle rose, holding a hand out to Simon. "Shall we?"

He didn't answer before an explosion rocked the boat, shattering the window beside him.

The boat pitched and knocked Gabrielle down.

Three more explosions followed in rapid succession splitting the floor of the passenger cabin. Water burbled up in the cracks, but it was quickly replaced by smoke and flames.

Simon's hand reached out into the aisle, and Gabrielle stretched toward it before her vision went dark, her final thought a realization that they weren't going to make it to the wedding.

THINGS CATS PUT IN THEIR MOUTHS

I closed and locked the door to my apartment before I took the garbage out, I'm sure of it. And there's no one home to let one of the cats out into the hallway. But Jiji, my jet-black kitty, is sitting just to the right of the apartment door, licking his paws.

His tongue flickers out, something bright, neon pink across it. It's probably a thread, shed by the laundry.

I scoop him up with one arm and try to sweep his mouth with the opposite hand, but he turns his head away from me and yowls.

Unlocking the door to let us in, I don't let him hop out of my arms once we're inside. Instead, I set him on the counter and try to scruff him so I can get a better look at whatever he's found.

He squirms when I grasp the loose skin behind his head, then hunkers down, turning his face away from me.

Whatever it is, the ends aren't hanging out of his mouth, so it must be just a scrap of string. But even that might cause problems, so I tug at his lower jaw as I tip his head back, trying to see the thread.

I get a hiss out of him in exchange.

But I don't see anything in his mouth.

"Don't you dare cost me another car payment at the emergency vet," I mutter, letting him leap down from the counter.

His brother, Lune, the tabby, headbutts me in the back of the knee, his favorite way to let me know he'd like to be fed.

But as Jiji hits the floor, Lune bolts away, spooked, his striped tail puffed up to the size of a bottle brush.

"Play nice." I nudge Jiji with my shin as I grab a bowl from the cupboard and open the hard plastic container I keep the cats' dry food in since the incident when they devoured half the bag in one afternoon.

Lune is normally clamoring at my feet before I've set the bowl down, but Jiji must have spooked him enough that he's retreated to hide under the bed for a bit.

Meanwhile, Jiji sits at the near end of the hallway, again licking between his toes.

Again, there's that flash of something in his mouth.

I crouch and grab him mid lick, hoping to get a better look at it.

When I do, I notice the second black cat hunkered down at the far end of the hallway, eyes nothing but a thin rim of gold around huge black pupils, staring at Jiji.

I only have one black cat.

The Jiji beside me yowls, mouth wide open.

The bright pink thing isn't a string on his tongue.

It's an impossible shape, angles and joints unfolding and collapsing as I watch, growing larger as it climbs from his mouth like an impossibly thin crab flipped on its back and trying to right itself.

No, it's not something climbing out. It's attached, it's part of this creature that looks like a cat and charmed his way into my apartment.

I've seen enough horror movies to know how this ends.

I grab the false Jiji one-handed. It's one smooth movement as I open the door, toss him into the hall, and close and lock the door.

Not my Jiji, not my problem.

POSSESSION ROULETTE

It's cliché, but it's too quiet. It's like everyone is holding their breath. Which of us is possessed?

I look at the others in turn; they're each doing the same. It's not me. I'd know if I was harboring another soul.

Wouldn't I?

We're certain it's someone.

More than that, we're certain it's someone *else*.

But no one has spoken.

What if it didn't work?

No. The question should be: What if it worked too well?

No one speaks up. At a loss, we join hands.

The circuit completed, the soul is whole.

I am not possessed.

We are possessed.

"Possession Roulette" originally appeared in *Reach Your Apex*'s BlueSky feed, July 2025.

COCOON

a cozy cocoon,
like a full-body sweater,
wrapping all around

within, the bones shift,
transforming inhabitants,
seeking the next state

but a human-sized
butterfly is a horror,
mandibles too large

and no one would want
to shell out that butterfly's
supermarket bill

THE TOOTH FAIRY

What if the tooth fairy
also takes teeth
from animals,

presses their incisors and canines
against her edentulous gums,
and through her tooth fairy magic

takes on the form
of predators unmatched

and comes for your teeth next?

WATERSPOUT WRAITHS

There's a charge in the air,
lightning sparking ozone,
but something else, too—
an unsettled mood
and a darkened spot in the bay.

The water spirals,
dappled light and dark,
before it sprays and rises
into a full waterspout,
reaching for the clouds.

And within the vortex,
the grasping hands
of the drowned,
the deluged,
the damned,

reaching out, not up,
seeking a connection,
someone who can save them
from being once again engulfed
when the waterspout ends.

And though they yearn
for salvation,
or at least a reprieve
from their watersoaked weeping,
it never comes.

For the onlookers know
the unquiet dead,
the victims of the deeps,
are always angry,
never resting,

and though the spirits
want revenge,
one can't avenge
themself
against the sea.

ONLY CHILD

Bring your memories of loved ones back to the screen with Super8Converters! Just send us your old Super 8 films, and we'll send their contents back to you on DVD or Blu-Ray—your choice!

Lauren had tossed the stack of magazines the day she started cleaning out her dad's apartment. But the ad from the back of one had stuck with her.

When she found the box of Super 8 reels, a wave of nostalgia washed over her. So many of her childhood memories of her dad—and her mom's photos of him—had his Super 8 camera covering half his face, like a prosthetic lens through which to see the world.

"Richard, put that thing down," her mom would say. But a laugh always accompanied her request, and she primped and posed for the camera all the same.

Lauren sifted through the box, reading the dates on the worn cardboard boxes. They went beyond her birth, all the way back to her parents' honeymoon—she remembered a story about the camera being her dad's favorite wedding gift.

Setting the box on the only clear corner of the dining room table, the one where the magazines had been stacked previously, she pulled out her phone and searched for Super8Converters, the name she recalled from the ad.

Special bulk reproduction offer! Got more than fifty reels? Send them all in, and we'll process them for just $2.50 a reel! Got more than one hundred? Contact us for even better deals!

Lauren looked at the box, neat stacks of smaller boxes five by five. She picked the one out of the center and started counting the layers.

Five by five by five. A hundred and twenty-five memories in two- to three-minute chunks.

She sent an email to Super8Converters.

~

We can even repurpose the plastic reels, keeping them out of landfills! And your films will be processed, checked, and then destroyed, so you don't have to worry about someone else finding your precious memories!

Three DVDs arrived two weeks later. She marveled that the box she'd dropped off at a local facility could be condensed onto these three pieces of plastic. But she was glad to be rid of the volume of stuff her dad had accumulated. In the end, after she'd found all the sentimental items, she'd hired college kids to load everything else into a moving truck and take it to Goodwill. They'd asked if they could keep a few of his yacht rock records and a handful of ratty old flannel shirts, and she'd been more than willing to part with those.

The DVDs came with a typed list of which reels had been put on which DVD, along with chapter numbers so she could skip around. They'd ordered them chronologically, and she flipped through the list, noting the array of birthday parties and holidays over the years.

On the first page, though, one of the titles confused her. "Lauren and Lisa, one month old."

"Thank goodness you're an only child," her mom had said whenever Lauren had any sort of problem.

Why did this chapter have someone named Lisa in it, then?

She loaded the DVD, her cellphone in hand, halfway to calling her mom. But she paused. What if ...?

Bring your memories of loved ones back ...

She pressed play and skipped to chapter 23.

"Richard, put that thing away and help, will you?" her mom asked.

Her mom. Holding a crying baby in each arm.

Lauren recognized herself, the dimple in her chin she remembered from all her baby photos.

The other baby was hard to make out. Their face was scrunched up from crying, but it also seemed to blur and shift, as though her dad couldn't get the Super 8 to focus.

"Okay." One of her dad's hands came into view, reaching for baby Lauren.

"No, take Lisa. You can always calm her down."

The image spun for a moment, then landed on the side of Lauren's dad's face and the out-of-focus infant cradled one-handed against his shoulder. "Look at the camera, sweetie," he said, but Lisa could barely hold her head up, let alone turn to look at some clattering thing pointed at her.

Lauren's wailing had tapered off in the background, probably soothed now that she had her mom's full attention. But Lisa continued to cry, louder now.

"Oh, alright." With a click and an abrupt darkness, the home movie ended.

Lauren tapped her screen to dial. "Mom, was I a twin?"

~

Lauren knocked on her mom's front door, DVDs in hand. On the phone, her mom had insisted she had no idea what Lauren was talking about, and where on earth had such a question come from?

It seemed genuine enough, but Lauren couldn't shake the feeling that something was off about the entire situation. She didn't recall seeing the name Lisa on any of the boxes she'd taken to Super8Converters. But she'd sent them an email to see if they'd already recycled the boxes or whether they could check for the extra name on the labels.

... you don't have to worry about someone else finding your precious memories!

"I still have no idea what you were going on about, Lauren," her mom said when she answered the door.

"I brought the DVDs to show you. It's just weird, is all. But it's on this inventory list, and then, well, on the DVD, there's another baby."

Lauren's mom frowned as she read through the inventory list. "Only this one with an extra name and baby?"

"It's the only one I've watched so far," Lauren admitted, as she loaded the disc into her mom's DVD player. "But yeah, it's the only one on the list."

"Start with this one," her mom suggested, pointing to the chapter labeled "21, Lauren and Missy at the hospital."

Lauren nodded and navigated to the chapter.

The screen filled with a weary looking mother holding a newborn Lauren, face pink and cherubic, eyes closed.

"Richard," her mom said in the video, her voice pleading.

"Gotta capture this, Missy. She's perfect."

"She is."

"Lauren Elizabeth."

Her mom nodded. "Our little angel."

Lauren chuckled. "I guess all babies are angels when they're sleeping, huh?"

"You were pretty easy," her mom said as the DVD switched to the next chapter.

This one only showed Lauren, asleep in her crib, with her dad humming a faint lullaby. Just before the chapter ended, he said, "Someday, you'll be the big sister."

Beside her, Lauren's mom stiffened.

Lauren paused the DVD. "You okay?"

"Just an old memory," her mom replied. "Your dad always wanted more kids, but it wasn't in the cards. We tried, but—" She trailed off, staring at the screen with tears filling her eyes.

Lauren wrapped her arms around her mom. "I liked being your only child, Mom."

"Play the next one. I want to see this other baby."

Unpaused, the DVD jumped to Chapter 23, showing the home movie Lauren had watched earlier, her mom cradling two babies before her dad finally took Lisa into his arms.

As the video played, her mom shook her head repeatedly. "That's not ... I don't ... I remember your dad filming me when you were fussing like that, but there wasn't another baby. That's you, I can tell. But I have no idea where that other baby came from."

Lauren stopped the DVD. "Yeah. I don't get it. I'd say they accidentally gave us a recording of someone else's twins, but I can tell it's me too. I look just like my baby pictures. And that's obviously you. And dad's voice." She picked up her phone to check her email.

The email to Super8Converters had come back as undeliverable.

"No such domain name?" Lauren read. She opened the browser on her phone and typed in the URL.

It, too, came back as non-existent.

"This is weird," she muttered, frowning at her phone.

"Do you mind if we watch some of your birthday parties?" her mom asked. "I'd like to see something less weird after that."

Lauren nodded, setting down her phone. "Yeah, okay. And we can see if there's any other weird ones tucked in here."

~

Having watched all the chapters containing Lauren's birthday parties, they hadn't seen any other instance of the mysterious Lisa.

"I just don't understand it," her mom said.

"I mean, there are things people can do with video technology, adding in things that weren't there, or making actors look twenty, thirty years younger. I just don't understand why a video reproduction place would do that." Lauren sighed. "And maybe their website and email are just down today. I can try again tomorrow to get to the bottom of this."

"Alright, sweetie." Her mom hugged her at the door. "Love you."

"Love you too, Mom."

"Maybe," her mom began. "Maybe just put those DVDs away. You're still going through a lot of grief over your dad passing. I am too, honestly. Even though we weren't married any more, he still was a good man I loved once upon a time."

"Yeah," Lauren said. "You're right. Grief does funny things to our heads." She hugged her mom again.

~

Lauren was ready to follow her mom's suggestion and put the DVDs away as soon as she got home.

She wasn't expecting a basket at her apartment door.

Especially not a basket containing a sleeping infant.

"What the hell?" she asked, backing away.

But before she had, she'd identified the cursive embroidery on the blanket covering the infant.

It said Lisa.

Bring your memories of loved ones back ...

WITCH KNIGHT

I wanted to learn magic for my protection. Our teachers insisted there was insufficient time for knights to train in combat and magic. But they told stories of sorcerous knights, so there were ways.

I traded sleep for research. I found tantalizing pacts offering what I sought. The church warned against demonic deals, while telling us angels could fall, becoming demons.

So how bad could it really be?

Some demons begin evil, not as fallen angels. They're the ones most likely to offer their "protection" to the desperate, aspiring witch knights.

Now I have my protection, but at what cost?

"Witch Knight" originally appeared in *Hawthorne and Ash*, January 2025.

DARE

The old bridge across the ravine had dwindled to a single rope, like a sad, worn tightrope. Nearby, an owl's ominous hooting punctuated the tense silence.

Laura wished she'd been brave enough to say no to her college friends. But a dare was still a dare, even now.

With a deep breath, she slid one foot out along the rope, which creaked in response. Precariously balanced, she lifted her other foot from solid ground.

The rope disintegrated beneath her foot. She grabbed at a stone block that had been part of one end of the bridge, but it crumbled away from the dirt as though it had been holding on through sheer stubbornness alone.

Her friends, watching, gasped as Laura fell screaming into the ravine.

Their gasps turned to screams when Laura's cries ended abruptly, as she plummeted straight into the massive maw of some monstrous creature lurking below, which swallowed her whole.

They didn't stop to see what else happened. They ran, never to return.

Though they did discourage everyone at the university from daring anyone to attempt to cross the ravine in the campus woods.

TAROT ESOTERICA: THE BLACK LAGOON

One of the least-known cards of the *Tarot Esoterica*, the Black Lagoon represents an emotional morass with no clear way out. Nicknamed the "longest depressive episode" card by some practitioners, its interpretation can be a delicate balancing act, as it indicates the querent is experiencing difficulties, but the engulfing miasma of the Black Lagoon offers no easy escape.

When reversed, the Black Lagoon continues to represent the same swampland, though the writhing vines and kudzu that stretch upward may be even more constrictive than the sucking quagmire.

Skilled practitioners often gloss over this card, hoping the querent will do similarly.

"Tarot Esoterica: The Black Lagoon" originally appeared in *Hawthorne and Ash*, January 2025.

THREE YELLOW FLOWERS IN THE BOTANY LAB

The yellow flowers don't look alike when they're blooming. After they're dried, it's easy to mistake one for another. It's why Jessamine carefully labels each sample, especially her namesake flower.

When the wind gusts, knocking out the power and startling her, and the tray is swept off the table, the dried blossoms mingle with glass in a nondifferentiated mess. She should sweep them up, but she reaches for one instead.

Her thumb finds a glass shard hidden within. Now she wishes she'd kept them in separate trays, as she waits to learn which deadly toxin is seeping into her veins.

"Three Yellow Flowers in the Botany Lab" originally appeared in *Reach Your Apex*'s BlueSky feed, November 2025.

GLITCH FOG

Carnivals were supposed to be fun. And a carnival that ran late into the evening was practical, so people who couldn't take time off work wouldn't miss out. That had been Meredith's thought process when she'd suggested the night carnival to Jack for their second date, after a traditional dinner and a movie on their first date.

He'd been enthusiastic. It wasn't until they arrived that she realized he'd invited a bunch of his buddies to meet them there. That only one of those buddies brought his girlfriend suggested this wasn't a group date, this was a chance for the guys to hang out and drink beer while the two women perhaps awkwardly bonded. Or perhaps she was the only girlfriend of the bunch.

Meredith wished she'd insisted on driving herself, rather than getting a ride with Jack. If she had, she could leave now and chalk this up to another stint of ineffectual online dating.

She looked at the menu above the bartender's head, wishing it had something resembling a mixed drink she could order without the alcohol. She wasn't opposed to hanging out and drinking, but the carnival was in the middle of nowhere, down dark, windy roads, and she wasn't looking forward to the return drive. Perhaps she could convince Jack to give her his keys now, before he got too much drunker.

The bartender leered at her, or at least it felt like a leer, with his too-few-teeth smile and lazy eye. "Getcha anything?"

"No, thank you." Turning back toward the guys, she said, "I think I'm going to go check out some of the rides."

"Ooh, can I come with?" Meredith couldn't even remember the other woman's name, as it had been part of the blur of meeting six of Jack's friends all at once. It started with a C or a K maybe? Carrie? Karen?

Meredith nodded. "Sure! We'll meet you guys back here later!"

One of the guys—Peter, Meredith thought—chugged his beer and lurched forward. "Hey, wait, Cassie, I'll come with too."

Cassie shook her head. "No. I don't want you puking on me on a ride. Go get some popcorn or something and sober up."

Peter's shoulders slumped, but he nodded. At least he seemed a little more sensible than the others, who were now trying to fashion a beer bong out of snow cone holders and a roll of duct tape they'd found somewhere.

As they walked away, Cassie said, "Sorry Jack dragged you along for this nonsense."

"Eh, it was my idea to come here. I didn't know it was a group outing."

"Yeah, they've been coming to the carnival for years to get wasted. The good news is I've got a cousin with a huge old Victorian house within walking distance, and the carnival doesn't care if we leave the cars parked here overnight. So I let them have their fun and herd them all over to Walt's house to crash afterward."

"Oh." Meredith was a little unsure what to think of Jack's ready agreement to the carnival now. If he'd been on many of these excursions, he must have known they'd end in spending the night nearby, which suggested he might have been doing this as a ploy for sex. And Meredith wasn't about to have sex with him tonight, given how drunk he was. If the house was big, like Cassie said, she'd have to find a spot to sleep that wasn't beside Jack.

"Anyway, what kind of rides are you up for?" Cassie asked.

"Anything, but I'm eyeing that carousel."

The carousel sat atop a natural rise in the ground, all twinkling lights and faint music above the dimly lit walkways of the rest of the carnival. It looked peaceful, an oasis above the wild rides and louder music and drunken groups of twenty-somethings like the one Meredith and Cassie had left behind.

"Sweet," Cassie replied. "I didn't want to suggest starting with a kiddie ride, but I'm a fan of anything that doesn't seem like it's going to make me feel as drunk as the guys are getting."

Meredith nodded. "They're not going to get like ... puke all over everything drunk, are they?"

"Not if they can help it, no. To some of them, puking is a sign of weakness. So if any of them starts feeling pukey, they head for some privacy—outside, or the restroom."

"Ugh, machismo." Meredith groaned, but it turned into a chuckle. "I don't mean to lump your boyfriend in with that. How long have you been dating?"

"Five years. I've known them all since high school, but Peter is slightly less of an idiot than the rest of them. He tells me he's lucky to have found me and not chased me away with his antics."

The two women had reached the carousel, where a bored teenager leaned against a podium that looked like it might have been salvaged from a church. Up close, the carousel music sounded a lot more like pop with vocals than the usual circus-themed calliope music on this sort of ride.

When the teen spotted them, she straightened quickly, eyes wide, as she fumbled for what turned out to be a remote control. She aimed it at the carousel and pressed a button, and the normal carousel music came back. "Hi, are you here to ride?"

Cassie nodded. "And we don't care if you keep the other music on. Is that the new Seven Ways from Sunday?"

"Yeah, good ear. But management wants us to play the proper music for guests."

"Oh well." Cassie scanned the ride, which was slowing to a stop. "Okay, are you a unicorn, tiger, or llama girl?"

Meredith shrugged. "Whichever one you like."

"C'mon, you have to have a preference."

"Well, I've never ridden a llama before. Real or carousel."

Cassie chuckled. "Llamas it is, then."

"I think they're alpacas," the ride attendant suggested.

"Llampacas it is," Cassie said with a shrug.

Cassie and Meredith climbed aboard side-by-side carousel animals. The wood saddles were smooth, well-worn, and not quite comfortable, but at least comforting.

"Hang on to your llampacas," the attendant announced over a loudspeaker on the carousel, as the ride began to turn.

Over a faint burst of static in the music, Meredith asked, "So, you've known Jack for a while. What do you think of him?"

Cassie shrugged. "I don't want to crush any dreams you might have of him being Mr. Right, but ... you know how some people think high school was the best years of their life?"

Meredith nodded, dread already creeping into her gut about what Cassie would say next.

"Yeah, that. I mean, maybe he just needs the right person to show him there's more to life after your glory days on the football field, but I imagine it'll take some patience."

Meredith nodded again. Cassie hadn't said anything horrible about Jack, but Meredith didn't think she was the right person to help convince a high school jock to grow up. She was patient, sure, but not *that* patient.

Instead of continuing the conversation, Meredith gazed out across the fairgrounds. The carousel had a commanding view of the area, though most of the landscape beyond the carnival was now shrouded in fog. Only the lights of the booths and attractions below held back the fog's creeping tendrils, and they were losing that battle.

"How hard is it to get to your cousin's house from here?" Meredith asked Cassie.

"It's an easy hike, fifteen minutes, max."

"What about in the fog?"

Cassie peered past Meredith. "That's what God made cellphone flashlights for. But I suppose we should corral the boys sooner rather than later. Wouldn't want any of them twisting their ankle in a gopher hole."

The ride began to slow, but the attendant's voice came over the carousel loudspeaker again. "Nobody else in line. Want to ride again?"

Meredith glanced at Cassie and smiled. "Sooner rather than later. But I wouldn't mind another ride."

Cassie nodded, then called out to the attendant, "Play it again, Sam!"

A thump a moment later rattled the carousel platform, and soon after, the ride attendant appeared and swung up on a nearby polar bear. "It's Arwen, actually."

"Like from *Lord of the Rings*?" Meredith asked.

"Yep. My parents are big fans," Arwen replied.

"Nice. I'm Meredith, this is Cassie."

"Cassie Steeple, right?" Arwen asked.

"Yeah?" Cassie said, eyeing Arwen.

"My cousin Felicia was in your grade, I think," Arwen said.

"Oh yeah, I remember Felicia! How's she doing?"

Meredith tuned out of the conversation. The folks in this area loved seeing how they might know each other or be related to one another. The nice thing about being from out of town was people didn't know her or her relatives. But it did cut her out of conversations occasionally.

Turning her attention back to the fog, she realized the rest of the carnival was almost smothered by the white blanket that had lingered at its edges a minute or two earlier.

"Umm, Cassie? Arwen?" She gestured out from the carousel. "Is this normal around here?"

Arwen blinked a couple of times as she took in the fog. "Nope."

"Definitely not," Cassie said.

Arwen slid off the polar bear and leapt from the edge of the carousel, hitting the ground at enough of a run to keep from falling. As she did, static overwhelmed the carousel music.

With the static, the fog jolted into angular shapes, like something made from pixels at a low resolution.

"What the—" Cassie began.

"You saw that too?" Meredith asked.

"Yeah. Like, blocks. Or ice cubes. Fog doesn't do that."

The carousel slowed, and when the attendant's booth came into view again, Cassie and Meredith leapt down to join Arwen, who was staring down toward the fog. "Did you guys see it glitch?"

Meredith nodded. "It happened when the music went staticky."

Arwen rolled her eyes. "Yeah, piece of crap old CD player playing the music for this thing. I think there's a scratch or something on the CD."

The CD skipped again, as if to emphasize the point, and the fog responded as it had previously.

"It's getting closer," Cassie said, her voice quiet.

Arwen shook her head. "Fog never rolls up this high."

"Maybe normal fog doesn't, but this doesn't seem like normal fog," Meredith said, matching Cassie's quiet tone.

Arwen picked up the remote on the attendant's stand and pressed a couple of buttons, then pressed and held a third button. The opening strains of the pop music she'd been listening to when Meredith and Cassie had arrived at the ride began pouring from the carousel's speakers, louder than the calliope music had been.

The fog creeping up the hill recoiled, as though the sound was too much for it.

"That's not normal either," Cassie whispered, barely audible over the loud electric guitars and drums.

"Guess it doesn't like nu-emo," Arwen said.

"Can we move the CD player?" Meredith asked.

"You aren't thinking about going down there, are you?" Cassie asked.

"It's either that or stay up here until the fog leaves," Meredith replied. "And I don't know about you, but I'd rather get out of here and far away from this creepy fog."

The music fuzzed into static, and the fog glitched again. This time, a space cleared in one of the carnival fairways below, and within it, blocky bodies moved, having the same angular, pixelated form the fog had taken on.

When the music resumed its melodic drone, the fog again became amorphous, and the people smoothed back into their normal shapes.

Arwen screamed.

Meredith wrapped an arm around Arwen's shoulders, though her eyes were wide. She tried to disbelieve what she'd seen, but Arwen's screaming suggested the oddness wasn't limited to her vision. "Shhh, it's okay, we're going to get out of here."

Arwen shook in Meredith's grasp. "Yeah, okay, sure. Uhh. Noise. It doesn't like noise. Oh. The CD player isn't portable."

"How loud can it play?" Cassie asked.

"The speakers can handle less volume than it's probably capable of." Arwen calmed with something else to think about. "Give me a few minutes, and I'll see how loud I can get it without distortion."

As Arwen leapt onto the unmoving carousel, Cassie looked at Meredith. "Jack said you're pretty smart. Any good ideas?"

Meredith chuckled. "I'm a data analyst. I guess that's smart by some standards. But I don't think it's particularly meaningful when you're dealing with an unnatural fog."

"But it might have rules, right?" Cassie asked.

"Maybe? It doesn't like loud music, but if there's static or a pause or something, it turns extra weird." Meredith paused. "And it's, well, glitching when the music up here skips, even though I don't think it should be loud enough to be heard down there. We couldn't hear what Arwen was listening to while we were walking up here."

Cassie nodded. "Right. So it reacts to sound waves the human ear can't pick up?"

"That's possible," Meredith said. "Vibrations, maybe. When they're patterned, it's fine, but when they're unpatterned, the fog reacts?"

"So it's the opposite of that *Dune* thing about walking and worms. If we go down there stomping rhythmically and loud, maybe the fog will stay away and not glitch out?"

Meredith looked at the nearest tendrils of fog and began stomping her feet like she was marching in place.

Cassie watched Meredith, and once she was nodding along with the rhythm, she began to stomp as well.

"What are you guys doing?" Arwen called from the carousel.

"Testing a theory." Cassie turned in place beside Meredith. "How's the CD player?"

"Turned up all the way already."

"And there's no volume control for the speakers on the carousel?"

"If there is, I don't know where it is. The remote they gave me only controls the CD player itself."

"They could be at full capacity too," Meredith said. "I don't think marching is doing the trick, Cassie. So it's volume, not vibrations."

"But that doesn't explain why the fog glitched when the CD skipped."

"I know, but it's the one constant in this. When the sound isn't right, the fog isn't either." Meredith frowned. "Arwen, the CD player, it's got cables of some sort connecting it to the speakers?"

"Old school coaxial cables, with the exposed wires on the ends, like my grandparents' stereo had."

Meredith winced at Arwen's definition of "old school" being associated with her grandparents. She'd grown up with the style of coaxial cables the teen was talking about. "So that won't connect to our phones."

Arwen laughed aloud. "Hell no." She paused and dug around in the podium where the carousel controls were housed. "But a phone in a cup works as a makeshift speaker, right? Maybe we could get it loud enough if we all have the same song on our phone?"

Meredith eyed Cassie and Arwen and shook her head. "I've mostly got instrumental movie soundtracks."

"I've got a little bit of everything, but it's mostly pop and country, honestly," Cassie said. "I haven't bought the new Seven Ways from Sunday."

"There's no signal out here strong enough to download anything new." Arwen scrolled through her phone. "I've got one T. Swift song." Her phone began playing a song, and she angled the cup she'd placed it in toward the fog. Even as she increased the volume, nothing changed with the nearest fog bank.

"Try some different songs?" Meredith suggested.

Arwen nodded and switched to a few different songs in succession. As the music got progressively more aggressive, the fog seemed to retreat from where the three women stood, but it barely cleared a space large enough for one of them to occupy, let alone all three of them.

Meredith scrolled through her phone, found the loudest, most bombastic song she had saved to it, and pressed play. As the two songs competed with one another for volume and ferocity, the fog glitched, like it had with the static.

"Whoa, no crossing the streams," Cassie said.

Meredith scrambled to stop the song on her phone. "Yeah, that won't work. It needs to be all the same, something harmonious and loud."

"Wait, I've got an idea. Something everyone knows. 'I've been walking around the same old town'." Arwen began to sing.

Meredith and Cassie both grinned in recognition of the classic rock tune and joined in on the song's next line.

As the three women sang together, the fog retreated from their voices, clearing a space wide enough for all three of them to press forward.

Meredith looped an arm through Cassie's, the other arm through Arwen's, and they began to march together down the hill.

As they walked, Meredith bit down her fear of singing in public. The goal was to be loud, not particularly good. Anything to keep the fog away, she reminded herself.

But her panic rose again when she recalled the song's lengthy guitar solo. She had no good way to signal to the other women what they should do at that point.

She didn't know how quickly the fog would move in if silence reigned, nor whether she'd be capable of coherent thought if they were surrounded.

As they reached the last line of the chorus before the guitar solo, a flash of inspiration hit her. Instead of singing that line with Cassie and Arwen, she stuck to the tune, but instead sang, "When we get to the solo, sing like the guitar!"

Arwen's eyes immediately lit up, and she launched into not only mimicking the guitar's whine but also released Meredith's arm so she could imitate the guitar player's strumming.

Cassie picked up on what they were doing, though she instead sang, to the tune of the solo, "We've gotta find the guys."

Meredith continued accompanying Arwen with her own imitation of the audible portion of the solo, though her lips drooped into a frown. Cassie was right, of course, but the fog was thick enough her plan might not be possible. "Do you know where they are?" Meredith sang, also matching the solo's tune.

Cassie sang only instrumental sounds, but she nodded once before her eyes went wide.

Meredith spun to look at Arwen, who was lost in her miming of the guitar solo but not the vocalization of it. Around her, the fog began to glitch across her arms.

With a yelp, Arwen came back to her senses, leaping toward Meredith and Cassie, and redoubling her efforts to sing the guitar solo rather than act it out.

Meredith took Arwen's hand and nodded to Cassie, who began leading them on a different trajectory.

They reached the final verse of the song and increased their volume as they sang the lyrics. Ahead of them, the fog parted, revealing Jack, Peter, and the rest of the guys, all looking as though they were going into shock, though not particularly cubic or glitchy at the moment.

Cassie released Meredith's hand, still singing, and grabbed the hands of Peter and one of the other guys.

Begrudgingly, Meredith dropped Arwen's hand to grab Jack's and a fourth member of the group, nodding toward the remaining guy and hoping Arwen would get the hint.

With his hand in hers, Jack seemed to come to his senses and started humming along with the song the women were singing.

Slowly, but surely, the other guys joined in the song, helping to clear an area of the fog large enough for all eight of them to spot the parking lot.

"When we get to the end, go back to the top," Meredith sang in place of the lyrics toward the end of the song. Cassie and Arwen joined her in repeating that line until everyone was nodding along with it.

"I've been walking around the same old town," Meredith sang as Cassie, Peter, and the other guy holding Cassie's hand passed through the carnival entrance. A moment later, she, Jack, and the fourth guy passed through as well, followed by Arwen and the last guy, hot at her heels.

Meredith turned to look at the fog. The carnival entrance seemed to hold it back, containing it from leaking out into the parking area.

Around her, the others trailed off in their singing.

"What just happened?" Jack asked.

Meredith eyed Cassie and then Arwen. "I think we escaped some dangerously unnatural fog." She shot Jack a quick glance. "I mean, it moved in fast, and we couldn't see through it. Singing was the best way to keep track of each other."

Cassie nodded, catching on to the story Meredith was spinning. "Yeah. We saw it roll in from the carousel and realized you guys would be lost without us."

"Ain't that the truth," Peter said, pressing his lips against the top of Cassie's head.

Arwen looked around awkwardly, as though she was suddenly aware she wasn't part of this group of twenty-somethings. "So, I should probably get home. I'm sure I can come up with some excuse why I didn't clock out."

"Or maybe never go back," Meredith murmured as the younger woman hugged her.

"Yeah, maybe that."

Arwen paused and looked back toward the fog, then turned back toward the parking area and walked toward the back corner of the lot.

In the dim light, Meredith couldn't be sure if Arwen's eyes had caught passing headlights in a strange way, or if they had glitched.

But she had to tell herself it had been the former. For it to be the latter was too much to deal with, and she'd already dealt with a lot tonight.

Thinking about that, she reached out a hand toward Jack, choosing her words carefully so he'd get her full meaning, that their second date was quite likely their last. "Seems like we should get out of here. Give me your keys, and I'll drive you home and call a cab for myself."

ABOUT THE AUTHOR

Dawn Vogel has written for children, teens, and adults, spanning genres, places, and time periods. More than 100 of her stories and poems have been published by small and large presses. Her specialties include young protagonists, siblings who bicker but love each other in the end, and things in the water that want you dead. She is a member of Codex Writers. She lives in Seattle with her awesome husband (and fellow author), Jeremy Zimmerman, and their cats.

Visit her at historythatneverwas.com or on BlueSky or Instagram @historyneverwas.

www.ingramcontent.com/pod-product-compliance
Lightning Source LLC
LaVergne TN
LVHW020047110826
845155LV00029B/671
9781948280495